THE DINOSAUR THAT POOPED THE PAST!

Check out Danny and Dinosaur in more adventures:

THE DINOSAUR THAT POOPED A PLANET!

Coming soon:
THE DINOSAUR THAT POOPED THE BED!
THE DINOSAUR THAT POOPED CHRISTMAS!

To the asteroid that wiped out the dinosaurs . . .
not cool, dude, not cool —T. F. & D. P.

For baby Kyle —G. P.

⚲ALADDIN

An imprint of Simon & Schuster Children's Publishing Division

1230 Avenue of the Americas, New York, New York 10020

This Aladdin hardcover edition March 2018

Copyright © 2014 by Tom Fletcher and Dougie Poynter

Illustrations by Garry Parsons

Originally published in Great Britain by Red Fox.

Published by arrangement with Penguin Random House Children's UK

All rights reserved, including the right of reproduction in whole or in part in any form.

ALADDIN and related logo are registered trademarks of Simon & Schuster, Inc.

For information about special discounts for bulk purchases, please contact
Simon & Schuster Special Sales at 1-866-506-1949 or business@simonandschuster.com.

The Simon & Schuster Speakers Bureau can bring authors to your live event. For more information or to book an event
contact the Simon & Schuster Speakers Bureau at 1-866-248-3049 or visit our website at www.simonspeakers.com.

Manufactured in China 1217 SCP

10 9 8 7 6 5 4 3 2 1

Library of Congress Control Number 2017932928

ISBN 978-1-4814-9868-5 (hc)

ISBN 978-1-4814-9869-2 (eBook)

THE DINOSAUR THAT POOPED THE PAST!

Tom Fletcher 💩 Dougie Poynter
Illustrated by Garry Parsons

ALADDIN

NEW YORK LONDON TORONTO SYDNEY NEW DELHI

Some grannies are old, some grannies are great,
  And Danny's was turning one thousand and eight.
He sang "HAPPY BIRTHDAY" with Dinosaur too,
  Then asked to go out: there was playing to do!

"You cannot go out till your plates are all clean!"
Said Granny while serving up sludge that was green.
So Dinosaur ate up Gran's hard Brussels sprouts.
Its head was quite free of all sprout-eating doubts.

And in the two seconds when Gran wasn't looking,
It ate Danny's pile of awful Gran-cooking.

"Well done!" Granny said. "You've eaten enough.
Now you can go out and do awesome cool stuff!"

They ran straight to the tree with a swing underneath,
But it hadn't been swung since Gran lost her teeth.
They swung back and forth; they went up, they went down.
"Higher!" Dan said. "Let's go all the way round!"

But this wasn't an ordinary swing; it had powers—
Powers to turn back the minutes and hours!
They counted to three and pushed hard off the ground.
They looped and they looped and they turned time around.

Their heads went all dizzy, time started to bend.
So Danny held on to his dinosaur friend!
Flashes and fizzes and sparkly squeaks,
They swung past the Romans, Egyptians, and Greeks.

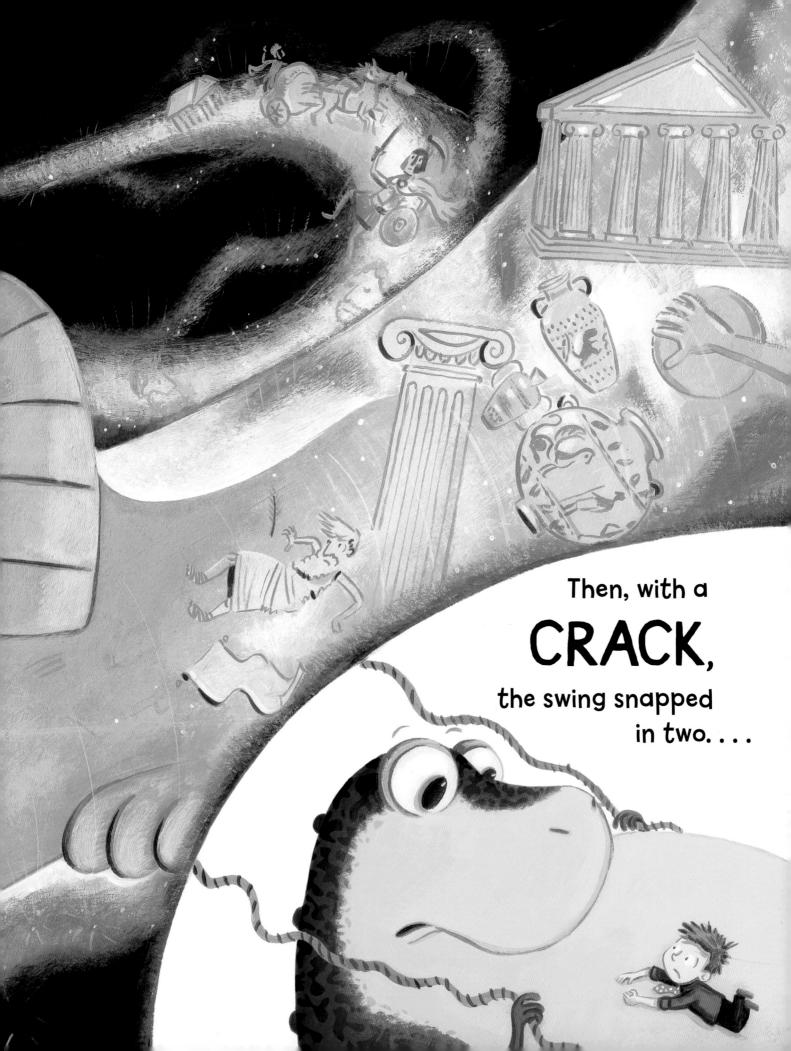

Then, with a
CRACK,
the swing snapped
in two....

And into the past Dan and Dinosaur flew,
Surrounded by trees of Jurassical size,
Being watched through the leaves by mischievous eyes.

Then three baby dinos jumped down awesomely,
Who called themselves Dino Dudes A, B, and C.
They liked playing games like stackety-stack,
Where Dino Dudes A and B climb onto C's back!

Then suddenly Dinosaur's
tummy made grumbles—
Grumbles and rumbles that
made the ground crumble.
But grounds do not crumble
for any old reason.
Grounds only crumble in
VOLCANO SEASON!

"We swung back in time; we were trying to play,"
Said Danny to Dino Dudes B, C, and A.
"We need to get back; we need to leave fast.
We need to get everyone out of the past!"

But Danny and Dinosaur's only way back
    Was looping through time on the swing that had cracked!

The lava was coming, the lava was hot—
    Even hotter than Granny's old sprout-boiling pot!

And so, without thinking, B, C, and A
    Stacked themselves up like the game that they play—
But this wasn't a game, it was saving the day.
    Saving the day the Dino-Dude way!

They flipped and they jumped through the jungle with ease,
Surfing the lava on lava-proof leaves,
Gathering all the things they would need
To fix the time-swing at the speediest speed!

Wax from the bees, sap from the trees,
    A tusk that fell off when an old mammoth sneezed—
They bashed it together with stegosaur teeth,
    While dodging explosive eruptions beneath.

The swing had been fixed, but the dinosaur group
Were now far too heavy to time-travel loop.
Dan started to worry, then started to panic—
The ground underneath was now hot and volcanic!

They all started crying; they cried and they cried.
They cried, and their tears instantly vaporized.

Then something in Dinosaur's mind went *ping*:
A new way to power a loop on the swing!

With broccoli eggs in the dinosaur's gut,
Its brain brewed a plan involving its butt.
It knew there was only one thing it could do—
To get back to the future it needed to . . .

POO!

The poop came out fast; it had broccoli power,
And launched them to eighty-eight miles per hour.
As Gran's soggy-egg meal came out of its rear,
Dino Dudes A, B, and C gave a cheer!

It pooped and it looped them
all forward in time,
Away from volcanoes,
and hot lava slime.

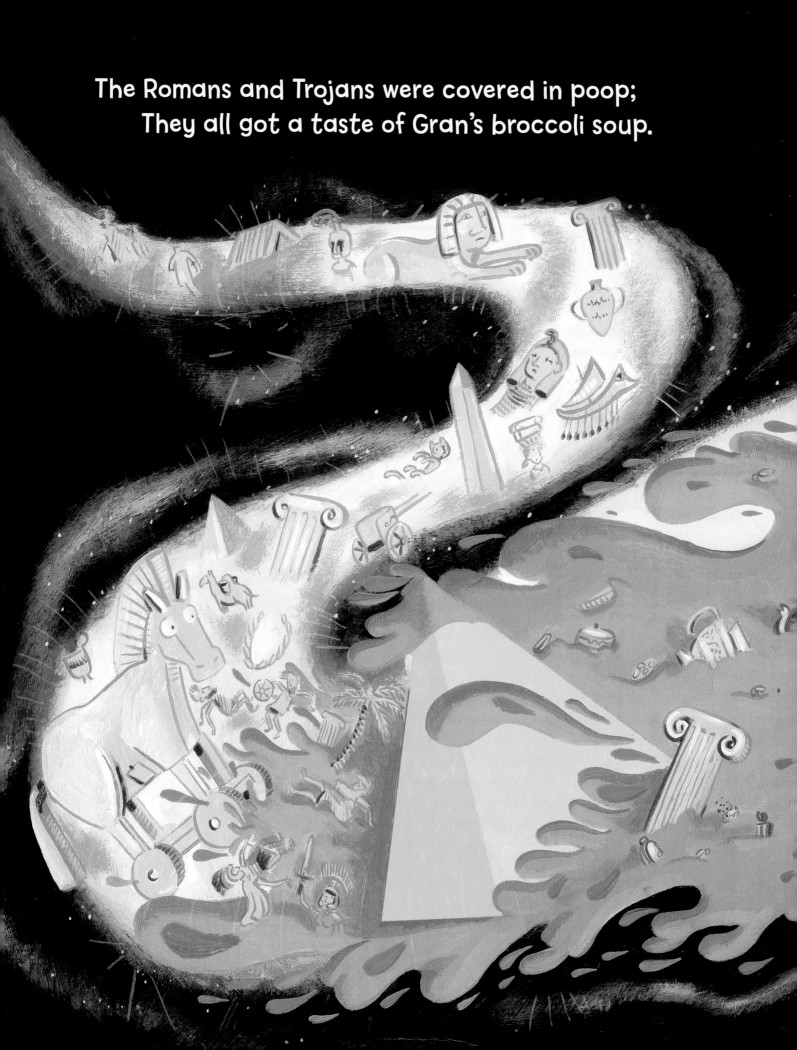

The Romans and Trojans were covered in poop;
They all got a taste of Gran's broccoli soup.

While looping through Egypt, it pooped out a pile,
Which made a poop pyramid next to the Nile.
It plopped out the sprouts, which smelled super smelly,
And looped out the last piece of poop from its belly.

They fell out of time, they'd made it back home,
  But Danny and Dinosaur weren't alone. . . .
Dino Dudes A, B, and C were there too—
  They'd traveled through time on the broccoli poo!

They all started cheering and jumping around.
It seemed like new dinosaur friends had been found!

And just when they'd had all the greens they could take,
Gran served her Brussels and broccoli cake!